HORSE DIARIES
· Risky Chance ·

HORSE DIARIES

HORSE DIARIES

Risky Chance

ALISON HART

illustrated by RUTH SANDERSON

RANDOM HOUSE NEW YORK

Text copyright © 2011 by Alison Hart
Cover art and interior illustrations copyright © 2011 by Ruth Sanderson
Photo credits: © Bob Langrish (p. 145); Library of Congress (p. 148).

All rights reserved. Published in the United States by Random House
Children's Books, a division of Random House, Inc., New York.

Random House and the colophon are registered trademarks of Random House, Inc.

Visit us on the Web! www.randomhouse.com/kids

Educators and librarians, for a variety of teaching tools, visit us at
www.randomhouse.com/teachers

Library of Congress Cataloging-in-Publication Data
Hart, Alison.
Risky Chance / Alison Hart ; illustrated by Ruth Sanderson. — 1st ed.
p. cm. — (Horse diaries ; [7])
Summary: In the mid- to late-1930s, Risky Chance grows from
a spirited colt to a winning racehorse, but an injury and the Great Depression
bring hardship that only a special little girl can help him overcome.
ISBN 978-0-375-86833-7 (trade) — ISBN 978-0-375-96833-4 (lib. bdg.) —
ISBN 978-0-375-89883-9 (ebook)
[1. Thoroughbred horse—Fiction. 2. Race horses—Fiction. 3. Horses—Fiction.
4. Depressions—1929—Fiction. 5. California—History—20th century—Fiction.]
I. Sanderson, Ruth, ill. II. Title.
PZ10.3.H247Ris 2011 [Fic]—dc22 2010027318

Printed in the United States of America

10 9 8 7 6 5 4 3 2 1

First Edition

To courageous racehorses and their brave jockeys

—A.H.

For Rob, the best horse trainer I know

—R.S.

CONTENTS

"Oh! if people knew what a comfort to horses a light hand is . . ."
—from *Black Beauty*, by Anna Sewell

HORSE DIARIES
· Risky Chance ·

1

March 1935

Run. Run. Faster. Faster. My hooves dug into the grass. My legs reached as I raced across the pasture. My ears flattened against my head, the wind blowing my black mane. I tossed a glance behind me. The other colts, my pasture mates, were far behind.

I neighed triumphantly as I wheeled in front of the white board fence. *The winner!* My friend Red Colt caught up. His eyes glittered, and he aimed a kick at my ribs.

I bucked with joy, almost knocking into Dark Colt and Bay Colt. They spun, and in a bunched herd, we thundered back to the gate.

Two men were leaning on the top fence board, watching us. I lengthened my stride, showing off, and inched past Red Colt, who snapped his teeth at me.

But his anger, his teeth, didn't faze me. Running, *winning,* were all I could think about.

Dark Colt and Bay Colt trotted over to the two men and earned a scratch behind the ears. I swerved, charging into the shed for a bite of hay. Curious, I peeked around the side. Now even Red Colt was standing quietly for a scratch.

Not me. No, sirree. I'd rather gallop to the other side of the field and see who's up for more fun.

In the next pasture, the fillies grazed peacefully. I bellowed at them, challenging them to race along the fence line. They nudged each other, but went back to their sweet grass. All except for Dappled Filly, who cantered toward me, accepting the challenge.

We sped down the fence line, neck and neck, neither of us gaining nor losing. When we reached the corners of our pastures, she swerved right and I swerved left. Every day we raced. Every day we were even.

Snorting, I cantered to the other side of the pasture. The mares, new spring foals by their sides, snoozed under the shade of an oak. Their field stretched from hill to green hill. Lifting my head, I called to my mother, a white silhouette against the blue sky. Last winter, she used to answer me. Now she ignored me, content with her spindly-legged black-haired foal.

When I was born, my coat was black, too. Now they called me Gray Colt.

Bored, I trotted back to my pasture mates. Maybe after the men left, I could goad them into another race. Sliding to a stop, I reared, snatching the air with my forelegs. Red Colt and Dark Colt skittered out of the way.

"That gray one's fast, but he's going to be

trouble to break," one of the men said. I recognized him as the human called Trainer.

The other man was as tall as a pine tree. "His sire's Risk Taker," he said. "His dam's Mary's Chance. Both were tough to train."

My ears pricked when I heard *Mary's Chance*. That was my mother's name!

"As I recall, neither did well on the racetrack," Trainer said.

Race! I knew that word, too. I pranced a little, bumping the other colts out of my way. I wanted to remind everyone that I was the fastest in the field.

"This colt seems to have the will to win," Tall Man said. "Some Thoroughbreds have it. Some don't."

Thoroughbred. I knew that word, too, because

it meant the horses at the farm. We were Thoroughbreds, bred to race, with large nostrils to suck in air and long legs for speed.

"The red colt's fast, too," Trainer said. "Man o' War's on his dam's side. And he'll be easier to break."

Break. There was that word again. I knew that branches could break and fence boards could break. I'd cracked one in half just a week ago, trying to jump out of my pasture to join the fillies. But how could horses break?

Not liking the idea of being broken, I ducked my head and hopped in place. Tall Man chuckled. "I like that gray colt's spirit," he said. "We'll see what happens now that he's a yearling. Tomorrow we'll start training."

Training. Ugh. I knew about training from

the two-year-olds. It meant staying cooped up in the barn instead of being free in the field. *No, sirree. Not for me.*

And the next day, when the humans called grooms walked from the barn carrying ropes and halters, I took off across the field. I watched from as far away as I could. They put the halters over the heads of Red Colt, Bay Colt, and Dark Colt. Soon my friends disappeared into the barn. Cantering back toward the gate, I whinnied frantically.

One groom stayed behind. He walked toward me, his arm outstretched, and I saw a carrot. I also saw the halter and rope he held behind his back. No treat was going to lure me close enough to get that rope slung around my neck. And since I was the fastest in the field, the groom would *never* catch me.

As he drew closer, I trotted away. We played this game until the sun started to sink behind the trees. By then, all the fillies had been led into the barn, too.

"Let him stay outside," Trainer finally called from the barn doorway. The groom left, carrying his halter, rope, and carrot. Then I was alone. Even the mares and foals were high on the hill and couldn't hear me neighing to them.

Night fell. Clouds gathered. The rain began in drips and drops. Then it burst from the sky in waves until my gray coat was slick.

Shivering, I slunk into the shed. As I pulled hunks of hay from the rack, I wished my friends were in the pasture with me. I wondered, *How will I be the fastest if there is no one to race?*

Through three storms, I stayed in the pasture. I raced from end to end, shooting mud in the air. Quickly I got bored with no one to beat. I hung by the gate, rain dribbling from my forelock onto my muzzle, listening to the sounds coming from the barn. When I whinnied, my voice sounded shrill and lonely.

Finally one day the sky turned blue, and the groom was again waiting by the gate. This time he held a bucket in his hand. Cautiously I stepped toward him, my hooves sinking into the soggy earth. I sniffed the air, smelling something sweet. Not sweet like mare's milk, spring grass, or fresh hay. This was different.

The groom began to whistle to himself. He

glanced up into the clear sky and then toward the mares and foals—looking everywhere but at me. I inched closer to the bucket. Lowering my head, I scooped up a few kernels before darting backward. As I crunched, the taste made my lips wiggle in delight.

"Like that grain, huh?" the groom said.

Dipping my head deeper into the bucket, I greedily grabbed a second bite. The rope slithered around my neck and tightened. The groom had caught me, but I didn't care. I *loved* grain—and I was tired of galloping across the pasture alone.

Gray Devil

May 1935

I hung my head in the back corner of the stall. Being locked up was worse than I'd heard. No sun on my face. No juicy grass to crop. No showing off for the fillies.

I still loved sweet grain, but it only came

twice a day. A groom dumped it in my bucket and then slammed the stall door shut. I couldn't even hang my head out and visit with the other horses.

Even worse was training. Different grooms led me around the barn. They shouted commands: *walk, whoa, back, pick up your hoof, quit kicking, stop biting.* There was no playing and bucking in the pasture. No racing until my lungs burned.

I wanted out.

Day after day, I patiently waited for my chance.

I heard the stall door open. A groom stepped in with a rope that had a chain at the end. This groom smelled like sweat. He was the one who barked like a farm dog when I balked and punched my muzzle when I tried to bite.

Cocking one back leg, I eyed him without turning my head. He saw my raised hoof. "So you want to kick me, Gray Devil? Ain't going to happen." Leaving the door open, he avoided my hind end and made his way along the wall toward my head. He reached out with one hand to clip the chain to my halter ring.

I spun so fast, I knocked him into the corner before bursting from the stall. I charged down the aisle, darting around Red Colt, who was being brushed.

The groom rushed from the stall, shouting angry words. I headed for the open barn door, neighing to the other colts and fillies. *Run away with me! Escape!* I heard their excited whickers and the raps of their hooves on their doors.

"Whoa, whoa!" other grooms hollered as

they got into the chase. Trainer poked his head from a doorway as I sped past. Full of daring, I raced from the barn into the sunlight.

Tall Man was stepping out of his car. A look of astonishment spread over his face as I galloped by him. With the wind in my mane, I flew down the roadside.

I'll never stop running until I'm far away.

The road wound between the fenced fields. As I slowed to a canter, I spied Mother. All the mares raised their heads to stare curiously at me. Several trotted over to find out what was going on, their foals hugging their sides. Mother only shook the flies from her face and continued to graze.

I halted and snuffled noses over the top board, making several mares squeal. They kept their babies away from me, shielding them with their bodies. Lead Mother turned her haunches and kicked in my direction, signaling *go away*.

Then I heard a roaring sound by the barn. I cantered off, but the roaring sound grew louder as two trucks came after me.

I sped up, racing the trucks as they pulled

alongside me. Ahead, the white board fences ended and a green field high with grass beckoned. If I could reach that field, I could run forever.

Trainer poked his head out of an open window in one of the trucks. "He's goin' thirty-five miles an hour!" he hollered. The truck shot forward, followed by the second one.

No! They can't win! I pushed myself, my legs moving so fast they must have been a blur. My heart was bursting, but I had to beat them and reach the field beyond.

In front of me, the trucks slowed. They swung around and parked between the two fencerows, blocking the way. Grooms jumped from the trucks, placing themselves so I could no longer see the green fields of freedom.

I slid to a halt. Trainer, a rope and bucket in his hands, got out of the truck along with Tall Man. They stood before me in the road.

My sides heaved. My breath blew. I *wasn't* going to be caught.

We stood there, not moving. Finally Tall Man took off his hat and slapped it against his leg. "Did you see that colt run?" he exclaimed. "Did you clock his speed?"

"He does have grit," Trainer agreed. "Except none of my men will work with him anymore. He's kicked, bit, or knocked down every one of them. Sure, he can run, but if we can't get a bridle or saddle on him, we'll never get him in a race."

"Let's geld him and then turn him out with a couple of feisty mares," Tall Man said. "In a month, we'll start over and see what we've got.

This time I want one man to work with him. Your best person, got it?"

Trainer nodded. "Yes, sir."

"I've registered him with the Jockey Club," Tall Man said. "My first pick for his name is Risky Chance."

"Risky Chance," Trainer repeated. "I believe that name fits him. He's going to be risky to train."

"But if we take a chance on him, we're going to see him in the winner's circle."

I had no idea what Trainer and Tall Man were talking about. But that day, as I reluctantly trotted away from the green field and back toward the barn, the trucks following behind me, I vowed never to let anyone beat me in a race again.

July 1935

The grooms called them Mabel, Sweetie, and Angel. I called them Grumpy Mares. For many nights and days I had been living in their pasture. Too old to have foals any longer, they ruled their field with swift kicks and sharp teeth. They hogged the best grass, the buckets of grain, and the shadiest spots. I tried my best to avoid them, but they delighted in pinning me in a corner and "putting me in my place." Soon my neck and flanks were slashed with cuts and scars.

A groom came once a day to check water and bring grain. But since the field was tucked behind the barn, no one else came around. There were no fillies to race, no colts to play with, no grooms to tease. This, I realized, was worse than training.

Finally, one hot day, a man opened the gate

and walked into the field. A red apple shone in his palm. The mares were resting in the shed away from the flies, so they didn't see him. I was near the gate, frantically stomping a pesky bug. Eyeing him, I blew in his direction. This groom had dark skin and a gentle smile, and I was so delighted to see a friendly face that I hurried over to greet him.

"Hey, boy, you ready to join the other colts and fillies?" he asked as I crunched the apple. He rubbed under my forelock. It felt so much nicer than the pinch of teeth that I stepped closer.

"Name's Lanny. I hear they call you Gray Devil," he said as he continued to scratch. Stepping back, he inspected my scars. "Looking at your sorry hide, I think the mares may have knocked some of that devil right out of you."

I nudged him in the shoulder, wanting more rubbing.

He chuckled. "You agree, huh? From now on, I'll call you by your given name, Risky Chance. Chance for short. That okay?"

The scratching and the kind sound of his voice were more than okay. Still, when he snapped the rope to my halter, I skittered sideways. Memories of training filled my head. Then Grumpiest Mare came ambling in our direction, and I almost ran Lanny over trying to get through the gate.

He led me into the barn, which was dark and cool, with no flies. I spotted Red Colt in his stall and greeted him with eager snuffles through the bars in the door. Then I moved to the next stall, where Dappled Filly whickered excitedly.

Instead of yanking me away, Lanny let me talk. We hadn't forgotten each other, and I realized how much I had missed our races.

Lanny put me in a stall between Dappled Filly and Bay Colt. I walked round and round, touching my nose to my own water and grain buckets and pile of hay. While I ate, Lanny groomed me, running the brush lightly over my rough coat before applying something soothing to my cuts, scars, and bug bites. While he worked, he hummed, which sounded as pleasant as the bees around the flowers.

A few of the other grooms stopped to look inside. I pinned my ears at the one who smelled of sweat. "Gray Devil looks like a scarecrow now," he said.

"Let them call you scarecrow," Lanny said

when the man left. "I been watchin' you. You've got balance and speed. We've just got to make sure your training goes right this time."

Flipping one ear back to listen, I grabbed another mouthful of hay. For some reason, when Lanny said *training* it didn't sound like yanking, slapping, or yelling. It sounded more like an adventure.

"Then you'll find out what you were bred to do," he added, giving me a pat. "And that, Risky Chance, is running like the wind."

3

Training

March 1936

Lanny stroked my face. "It'll be all right, Chance," he told me. "Oscar's a pro at this."

Suspiciously, I rolled my eyes toward Oscar, a runt of a man who sat on my back in the saddle. One hand grasped my mane; the other held the reins.

I had been in training through the hot days of summer and the cool days of fall before again being turned out to run in the winter fields. By now, I knew how to load in a trailer, pick up my feet for the farrier who trimmed my hooves, and stand quietly for the veterinarian, even when he pricked me with a needle. I now knew the bit, the saddlecloth, the saddle, and the girth. Lastly, I knew about riders. Oscar had ridden me round and round the area called the training track while Lanny led me. As long as Lanny was there, humming his songs, I didn't mind Oscar, even if he squeezed my sides with his legs or pulled right and left on the reins. But now I heard a click, and Lanny stepped away from me.

Oscar sucked in his breath. I puffed out mine. "I ain't too sure about this, Lanny," Oscar said. "This colt's full of fight, and he's not so scrawny anymore."

"He is plenty rugged," Lanny said in his calm way. "Give him a nudge with your heels. No kicks, now, or you'll send him sky-high."

Oscar steered me toward the railing that circled the outside of the training track. As I

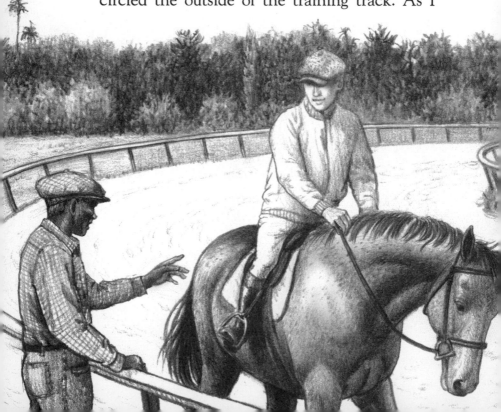

walked, two colts trotted past me. Riders moved up and down on their backs. I pricked my ears to watch them. These colts were older than I was. Their necks were arched, and their haunches churned with power. "They're ready to race," I had heard Lanny say the other day. "Ready to go south to Santa Anita."

Tossing my head, I danced in place. My heart began beating faster. I didn't know the words *Santa Anita*, but I was ready to race.

Oscar chuckled. "Chance is eager to go, Lanny," he called over his shoulder. "I can feel it."

"Bring him back, then!" Lanny hollered. "His knees aren't ready. He's got some more growing to do."

Oscar tugged on the left rein. I ignored him, my thoughts on galloping after those two horses, showing them that *I* was the fastest.

"Not yet," Oscar said. "Soon, though. Soon."

Reluctantly, I headed back to Lanny. He hooked the rope onto the bit ring. Oscar kicked his feet from the stirrups and jumped off. "Colt wants to race," he said.

"He does have what it takes to be a winner,"

Lanny agreed as he stroked my neck. My winter hair had shed out, and my gray coat shone. Raising my head, I continued to watch the colts. They'd broken into a gallop on the other side of the track, which riders called the backstretch. I could feel the pound of their hooves on the track, and I began to tremble with excitement.

All through that summer, Oscar and I worked on the track, until I, too, was cantering. Sometimes alone, sometimes with Red Colt by my side. One day, Oscar cantered me around the homestretch turn, which I had learned was the last turn before a pretend spot called the finish line. Lanny, Trainer, and Tall Man watched from the gate.

"Let him out at the three-eighths pole," Trainer called to Oscar.

Leaning forward, Oscar loosened my reins. Confused, I flicked my ears, not sure what he wanted me to do. Then he bumped me with his heels. Startled, I burst forward, and when he didn't rein me back, I sped up. Digging hard into

the track, I leaped in long strides until I was galloping.

Galloping!

I hadn't run this fast since last winter, when Dark Colt and I were turned out in the pasture to muscle up and grow. It felt exhilarating.

"Got it," Trainer yelled when I passed the imaginary finish line. Oscar sat deeper in the saddle and pulled on the reins. I shook my head, telling him *let me run!* But he steered me in a tight circle so the track no longer stretched in front of me, and trotted me back toward the waiting men.

Lanny was grinning as we walked up. Trainer and Tall Man were grinning, too.

"Three furlongs in thirty-three seconds," Trainer said as he studied something in his hand. "Not bad for the first time."

Tall Man let out a noise that sounded like a horse snorting. "Not bad? That's aces. Let's truck him to Santa Anita tomorrow. If all goes well, he should be ready to race in three weeks."

Ready to race. I heard those words again—and this time I pranced in place, knowing they were meant for me.

August 1936

Santa Anita. I finally knew what it meant. It was a giant place with a track bigger than the mares' field. It had rows and rows of barns filled with horses. Riders, grooms, and trainers darted everywhere like flies. And it had more noise, dust, and galloping than I'd ever known in my life.

Fortunately, Lanny came with me, and his quiet ways kept me from rearing, bucking, and bolting. After many days and nights, I got used to the confusing sights and smells. I loved having so many horses to whinny to, and I loved cantering around the track. Plus I met Barn Cat, who kept away the mice and slept in my stall.

Oscar didn't come with us, but Lanny chose a rider named Hughie, who had light hands on the reins and liked to hum, too. Lanny was careful to give Hughie directions on how to ride me, and even Trainer and Tall Man, who pretended to be the boss, listened to Lanny.

"Don't ever use your whip on this colt," Lanny warned Hughie. "If you do, he'll stop running for you."

So Hughie and I got along. We'd breeze down the track some mornings along with other sets of colts and fillies. Red Colt and Dappled

Filly weren't at Santa Anita, but I was stabled between Stakes Horse and Claim Horse. Stakes Horse, also named Jed's Dime, explained to me that he won lots of races for Tall Man, who praised him, fed him rich feed, and called him a champion.

Claim Horse, on the other hand, explained that after each race, a new owner might lead him off to a brand-new barn. Sometimes the grooms and trainers at the new barn were nice. Other times they were not. He disappeared from the barn before I even learned his name, so I decided right away that I wanted to be a stakes horse like Jed.

One morning, Lanny came early, even before I ate. "Chance, today you learn about the starting gate."

Lanny led me from the stall and over to a long gate that stretched almost across the track. Was this the starting gate? I'd seen horses walk into what looked like metal mouths in the gate and then charge out of the other side as if being chased. I wasn't too keen on learning about those mouths.

But Lanny had brought a bucket of grain. He hooked a long rope on my halter and led me close to a metal mouth. Then he walked through an opening carrying that bucket. I stopped short, my eyes buggy. He waited on the other side, humming.

"Come on, colt," he urged. "The chute ain't nothing to be scared of."

I locked my legs. Minutes passed. Sweat rolled down Lanny's cheeks. Gnats tickled my ears.

"Mmm-mmm." Lanny lifted a handful of grain and took a bite. "This sure is tasty."

My ears flicked. Was he eating my grain? I took one step, two steps—closer and closer toward the chute.

"Tast-e-e-e!" Lanny exclaimed, taking another bite.

Two more steps and I was right inside that mouth of a chute, metal rails on both sides of me. But my attention was on Lanny and that bucket.

Bounding through, I landed on the other side and thrust my head into the bucket. "Now that wasn't so bad, was it?" Lanny asked.

We practiced three more times, until I followed Lanny with no hesitation. The next day, we practiced with Hughie in the saddle.

"You just sit there," Lanny told him. "Let Chance walk through when he decides."

Well, no one had fed me breakfast that morning, so I decided right off not to wait—that grain needed to be eaten.

After that when we practiced, Lanny would stand farther and farther down the track. I'd have to walk into the chute, wait until Hughie chirped, then trot to Lanny. One day, he stood across the finish line. Instead of a chirp, Hughie gave me a poke with his heels. I shot out of that gate and cantered down the track. I could see Lanny on the other side. Ears pricked, I raced toward him, my legs stretching from a canter to a gallop. Suddenly, I was flying around that track. Flying around the backstretch turn.

Hughie was hunched on my neck, urging me with his body and hands.

Faster, faster.

I forgot all about that bucket of grain and Lanny. All I could think about was running. My spirits soared. I was free!

September 1936

Lanny led me into the barn aisle. I was tacked up, eager for my workout. Tall Man was there with Trainer. They looked serious. Hughie wasn't there, ready to ride me. Instead a man smaller than Hughie stood with them, his arms crossed.

"Meet Wolf," Lanny said to me. Barn Cat

wound between my legs, purring, as if wanting to meet Wolf, too. "Tomorrow's your first race, Chance. Wolf's gonna be your jockey."

Jockey. I knew it meant a rider who rode in the races. Throwing up my head, I stared at Wolf. Wolf stared back. Finally he said, "I've heard good things about you, colt. Word around the track is you're going to be the next Man o' War."

Lanny chuckled. "Chance sure acts like he's gonna be the next Triple Crown winner."

"Lanny picked you out, Wolf," Trainer said. "He thinks you're the rider to get the best out of this colt."

"You have one race to prove he's right," Tall Man added. "Chance is entered in the Santa Anita Chase. We expect results."

Wolf nodded. Lanny boosted him onto my

back. Barn Cat scampered into my stall as I set off down the aisle.

We wound through the shed rows down to the track. Lanny hummed as he walked by my side. Wolf sat quiet. I bucked a few times to test him. He didn't yank the reins or squeeze with his legs. Instead he placed a hand on my withers and stayed balanced in the saddle.

I broke into a bouncy trot as soon as I was on the track. A mounted attendant rode up. The attendant and his horse were there to help keep all the horses and riders safe on the track.

I skittered away from them, but Wolf stayed with me. I rooted my head, trying to pull those reins from his grasp. Rather than jerking back, he pressed his heels in my sides, nudging me into a canter.

We cantered down the track. I barely felt Wolf, yet I knew he was there. Somehow his hands and legs knew just what to say to me as we passed the other horses exercising on the track, too. He urged me with small chirps and words, and suddenly I knew what the word *jockey* meant: a rider to help me win.

It was the day of my first race.

Lanny led me round and round the saddling paddock with eight other horses and their grooms. Waves of humans surrounded the paddock, cawing and fluttering like crows. My nerves flared and I pranced sideways, but Lanny stroked my neck.

"This is it," he told me. "Your chance to do what you love. Your chance to show the world you're the fastest colt at Santa Anita."

The fastest. Yes, sirree. I knew what that meant.

Lanny halted me, and a man lifted my lip. Then Hughie put a saddle blanket the color of roses and dandelions on my back and, on top of that, a tiny saddle. Lanny tightened the girth. I spied Wolf striding toward me. He wore a roses-and-dandelions-colored shirt and cap. As he walked, he tipped his head to the humans

who waved at him from the railing. Suddenly,
a small person climbed over the barrier. She
wore a straw hat with a rose tucked in the
band. Shrieking, she launched herself at Wolf.
He scooped her up in his arms, though she was
almost as tall as he was.

"You're going to win today, Father," she said
when Wolf set her down. Turning, she stroked

my nose. Her fingers felt as soft as Barn Cat's fur. "May Chance have a carrot?"

"After the race, Marie," Wolf said. "Give me a good-luck kiss, and it's back to your mother."

Marie kissed him soundly on the cheek. Then she hugged me around the neck. The crowd laughed as I tossed my head in confusion. No one had ever hugged me before.

"You and Father *will* win, Chance," she said, looking up at me with serious eyes. "I *know* it."

"Off you go, Marie." Wolf pushed her in the direction of the crowd.

Lanny hoisted Wolf into the saddle. "Ride clean, and no whip," he told Wolf. "The colt will race to the front right off. Just sit chilly. This might be his first race, but I guarantee

Chance knows what to do to win. After the post parade, warm up with a light canter."

Post parade. I'd never heard those words before, and my head swiveled from side to side as a mounted attendant led the horses and jockeys in a line to the track. A roar from the crowd went up, and I snorted and hopped. The roar didn't frighten me. It *excited* me, and my body hummed with power.

Thousands of eyes were on us as I cantered down the track toward the starting gate. A noise like thunder erupted as we passed the grandstand. Music played. It wasn't soothing like Lanny's humming but clangy like banging buckets. Then one voice seemed to echo above the thunder and music, and I heard my name in the jumble of words.

When we were past the grandstand, I eyed the other horses. I recognized some of them from morning workouts. They were two-year-olds like me. Others were strangers. From all of them rose the smell of sweat and excitement.

Wolf nudged me to a canter, but then almost immediately sat deep in the saddle, signaling for me to walk. I had been so focused on the other horses that I'd forgotten he was even there. But when we reached the starting gate, I was grateful for his calm voice as a horse reared, narrowly missing me.

Then it was my turn to load. I pictured Lanny and his bucket of grain and walked right in. I stared down the length of the track. It stretched before me, smooth and empty. My feet danced in place, I was so eager to run.

A golden horse on my right and a brown horse on my left were just as restless. Down the line, a horse whinnied as if hurt. I smelled fear.

Wolf leaned forward. His fingers twined in my mane. I flicked my ears, feeling his energy.

Then a bell rang, and that same loud voice burst out, "They're off!"

Wolf brought his hands forward on my neck and kicked with his heels. I leaped from the starting gate. My hooves dug into the earth, propelling me forward. The golden horse and the brown horse broke at the same time as I did. Together, we shot to the front.

Wolf tugged lightly on the reins, signaling *take it easy*. But I didn't want to take it easy. I was back in the pasture galloping with Red Colt and Dark Colt. I knew then that I could beat both of my friends just as I knew today that I could beat these horses.

I raced around the first turn and down the backstretch. Slowly, I pulled away from the golden and brown horses. Easily, I galloped beside the rail. My lungs and nostrils filled with air: *puff, puff*. Blood fed my muscles, which were strong and lean.

Furlong after furlong ticked past as I sailed down the backstretch. Wolf turned slightly to glance over his shoulder. I could have told him

not to bother. I was far ahead of the other horses. I could no longer hear the pound of their hooves. I could no longer hear the smack of whips.

The only sound was my own breathing.

Faster. Faster. No horse was going to catch me today. As I flew around the homestretch turn, I wasn't running to beat the other horses. I wasn't running for the cheering people or for Trainer, Tall Man, or Wolf.

I was running because *this was what I was born to do.*

5

February 1937

Lights popped. Black boxes clicked. Humans wearing hats called to Hughie and Lanny, who sat on chairs on either side of my stall door. "When's he gonna work out this morning?" "Is Wolf riding him?" "Have they decided his next race?" "Is Mr. Davidson entering him in the Santa Anita Handicap next week?"

Snorting, I pawed my straw as the lights on the boxes popped, popped until I couldn't see. Barn Cat cowered in the corner of my stall as the shouting grew louder. Lanny and Hughie stayed silent.

Finally Tall Man entered the barn with Trainer. The Hats ran to meet them like mice scampering after my spilled grain.

Hughie grunted. "Wish they'd leave us alone. Why doesn't Boss hire a guard? We can't spend all our time babysitting just 'cause Chance is some big-shot horse that won eight races."

"You go on and get ready," Lanny said. I reached over to lip his cap, and he playfully swatted me away. "I'll tack up Chance. You're working him today."

"Where's Wolf?" Hughie asked.

"He's exercising a horse for Harrison."

Trainer and Tall Man walked down the aisle toward us, the Hats tagging behind.

"Chance has beaten the best colts and fillies in California," Tall Man was telling them. "We're definitely entering him in the Santa Anita Handicap."

"Chance might be fast, but he's no match for Seabiscuit," one of the men with hats said.

"And Rosemont is entered, too," another said. "The hundred-thousand-dollar purse is the largest in the world. Even the fast-talking own-ers back East can't resist it."

"We don't care about Seabiscuit or Rosemont," Tall Man said. He tried to pat me, but I ducked away. Tall Man's pats were hard thumps on my nose, and I didn't like them. "My money's on Chance. He's as sound as a Roosevelt dollar and ready to beat all entries in the hundred-grander."

When the people left, Lanny stood up. "Don't listen to those reporters," he told me as he put on my bridle. "For once Mr. Davidson is right: you are the best horse on the track."

"Chance!" someone squealed.

I pricked my ears toward the door. Marie ducked under the stall webbing. Her eyes were fierce. Red curls bobbled from under the brim of her fancy hat. "Those reporters are know-nothings. Seabiscuit and Rosemont might be fast," she said, "but they aren't as fast as *you*."

She held out her hand. I carefully plucked a slice of carrot from her fingers. "Father says that you have more heart than any horse he's ever ridden."

"You got that right, Miss Marie," Lanny said as he saddled me. "And he has something else special the other horses don't have."

"What?" Her eyes grew wide.

Lanny chuckled as he led me from the stall. "You and your hugs."

Hughie was waiting in the aisle, boots on, and Lanny boosted him into the saddle. Marie gave me one last hug.

Soon we were on the track for an easy workout. Rain had soaked the ground, but I didn't mind mud squishing under my hooves.

As I trotted along the rail, I spotted Marie. She waved at me from her perch on the outside railing where she watched. Then I spotted her father. Wolf was in front of us, trotting a filly. I could tell the horse was new to the track because she bounced from side to side, and her tail switched anxiously.

"Harrison put Wolf on some crazy two-year-old," Hughie said, steering me to the right. "Let's give her plenty of room."

Suddenly, a horse with no rider charged past us on the left. The reins flapped against his front legs, and the stirrups banged his sides. His eyes were white-rimmed, and he ran as if dogs were chasing him.

I jumped out of his way. As he flew by, hugging the rail, I sensed his fear.

"Loose horse!" Hughie hollered.

Wolf threw a glance over his shoulder. But it was too late. The riderless horse ran smack into the filly. She leaped into the air, flung her body sideways, and landed on the rail. I dug in my hooves, sliding so fast in the mud that Hughie lurched onto my neck.

Legs flailing, the filly flipped over the railing, Wolf clinging to her back. The wood cracked, and I heard someone scream. I glanced toward the outside railing. Marie was leaning over it, staring in the direction of her father.

Hughie screamed, too. He kicked me forward, but I wouldn't budge. Already the mounted attendants were cantering over. Grooms and workers sped toward the broken railing.

I stood frozen, shaking. On my back, Hughie seemed just as frozen.

The loose horse was still galloping down the track. A mounted attendant cantered after him, trying to head him off. Humans were shouting. A truck rumbled past me and stopped by the broken railing. I rolled one eye toward the out-side railing. Marie was gone.

Then Lanny was beside me, his palm on my neck. His eyes were red and watery. "Looks bad," he said to Hughie.

Without a word, he turned us away from the crowd that surrounded the broken railing. But as we headed back toward the barns, I could still hear Marie's screams ringing in my ears.

"Stubby's your jockey in the handicap," Lanny said a few days later. He was picking out my hooves. All day he'd been fussing over me, and that morning I'd gotten my special mash, so I knew it was a race day.

I poked my head over the stall guard, expect-ing Hats to be swarming like bees. The aisle was

empty except for Barn Cat watching a mouse hole.

Lanny chuckled. "No reporters today. They're bothering Seabiscuit and Rosemont. But that's good for us, colt. Odds are twenty to one on you, so no one believes you're going to win. That means money in my pocket when you cross that finish line first."

I snatched another bite of hay. *Finish line. Yes, sirree.* I knew those words well. I had crossed it ahead of every horse in every race. Why should this race be different?

But it *was* different. The air seemed to vibrate as Lanny led me to the saddling paddock. The crowd was so huge, they hung over the rails.

"There's Rosemont! There's Seabiscuit!" rang through the air.

I searched for Marie and her hug but couldn't find her straw hat and red curls in the crowd. Then Stubby strode into the paddock in place of Wolf.

Where was Wolf? Since the broken railing and the filly flipping, I often heard the word *accident*. But not one human at the track would say Wolf's name.

Lanny was frowning as he took the saddle from Stubby. Tall Man had chosen Stubby, and I knew Lanny didn't like the jockey. When he boosted Stubby into the saddle, the only thing he told him was, "No whip."

Then Lanny stroked my nose. "Sixty thousand people are here watching this race, colt. But you know what to do."

We headed from the paddock in the post

parade. I broke into a trot. Stubby took up the reins. *Too tight*, I tried to tell him by rooting my head. He only firmed his grip.

So I pushed Stubby out of my mind. I missed Wolf's light touch, but I also knew how to run and win without a jockey telling me what to do. I knew how to leap clean from the starting gate and charge to the front. That way mud and dirt didn't get kicked in my face. That way I didn't have to weave through the slow horses or get boxed in by crafty jockeys. And I always had a burst of energy in case a hotheaded runner tried to catch me.

I know how to win this race, yes, sirree.

I was the last to enter the starting gate. I danced in the chute, ready for the bell. Stubby was talking to the jockey next to him. "The track's like goo, Harry," he was saying. "Seabiscuit's got the worst footing in number three. We've got the best in seventeen and eighteen."

Just then, the bell rang. I was ready. Stubby was not. His fingers weren't twined in my mane, and when I shot from the gate, he fell back into the saddle. The bump threw me off balance. I went down, my front legs folding beneath me. Instantly, I leaped up and charged after the fleeing pack of horses.

Pain stabbed my front right leg. Stubby had righted himself. But we were lengths behind the last horse.

Ignoring the pain, I ran faster than I had ever run before. I flew past several horses that lagged at the back. Dirt clods pelted me as I galloped around the first turn. The other horses were packed against the railing, so I ran on the outside. Slowly, I gained.

Faster. Faster. I drew ahead of two more horses. Up ahead, I spied the area where Wolf had had his accident. The railing was fixed, but I *knew.* For a second, I hesitated.

Whap. Whap. I felt stings on my flank and heard smacks on my hide. Stubby had a whip.

Over and over, his arm rose and fell. I flicked my ears, trying to ignore the ache in my right leg and the slaps on my flanks. Tried to forget about the runaway horse and the filly flipping over the railing. Tried to think only about winning.

Run. Run. Faster. Faster.

Only five more horses ahead of me. *I can do it.*

Finish Line

I pummeled the track with my hooves. I charged past the middle set of horses and down the homestretch. The finish line was in sight. I was gaining on the front runners. Then, suddenly, the pain in my leg shot through me like fire, and I stumbled.

The crowd roared as the two lead horses crossed the finish line, neck and neck. Cries of "Seabiscuit" and "Rosemont" filled the air.

Gamely, I crossed the finish line, too. In an instant, Lanny was there. Grabbing my reins, he practically dragged me to a halt.

Anger twisted his face. He snatched Stubby's leg and jerked him from the saddle. "Why didn't you pull him up?" he screamed, shaking the jockey by the shoulders. "Why did you whip him? Couldn't you tell the horse was lame?"

"Hey! Hey!" Two men separated Lanny and Stubby. Then Trainer was there with the vet.

I was blowing, and my sides heaved. The pain made my eyes roll. Lanny tried to support me while the vet inspected my front right leg. "Feels like the colt bowed his tendon," he said, shaking his head. "Let's hope it's sprained and not torn." Rummaging in his bag, he pulled out padding and tape.

Lanny took off my saddle. After he threw it to Stubby, Lanny shoved him. Trainer and the vet had to hold Lanny back as the jockey hurried off.

Quickly Lanny stooped and wrapped my leg with padding and then taped it. He led me down the track, walking slowly while I hobbled beside him.

To my right, I could see the winner's circle crowded with people. A dark horse wore the blanket of roses. I saw the flashes and heard the shouting. "Rosemont! Rosemont!" rang out. This was the first time I wasn't the horse posing for the cameras. And as we passed by, no one was interested in me.

*   *   *

They sent me back to the farm, where Lanny tended me for many days and nights. He hosed my leg, iced it, rubbed medicine on it, wrapped it, and walked me. Slowly, the pain left. Slowly, I stopped limping.

And slowly, I forgot about Wolf, Marie, Santa Anita, and racing to win.

March 1938

Spring came and I was turned out in a small pasture. My leg felt good enough that I could canter along the fence line. I'd whinny at the yearlings, challenging them like in the old days. In the beginning, they would win. Then I began to beat them.

Oscar again started working me on the

farm's track. When I breezed, my leg felt strong, and the urge to run bloomed within me.

One hot day, Lanny came to the pasture where I grazed. His eyes glimmered as he stroked my nose before leading me into the barn. He groomed me as always, but there was no humming. When he was finished, he ran his gaze over me as I munched my hay. Then he shut the stall door and hurried away, his head ducked low.

I whinnied to him, but he didn't turn around.

I was finishing my hay when I heard people come into the barn. I popped up my head, hoping it was Lanny returning. But it was Trainer and a man shaped like a rain barrel.

"Winner of eight stakes races," Trainer was saying. "He's ready to win again."

Barrel Man grunted a laugh. "You mean

Davidson wants to dump him, so he's entering him in a claiming race at Tanforan."

Race! My ears pricked. I was going to race again!

Trainer shrugged. "Colt has a bowed tendon. It's healed, but the vet says it'll probably bow again. So yeah, Davidson wants to dump him but make some money, too."

"Gotcha." Throwing open the door, Barrel Man walked in with a lead line. There was no pat, no hello. He clipped the rope on my halter and led me out to a van.

I balked at the bottom of the ramp. Where was Lanny? Then I heard a whicker from inside the van. Dappled Filly?

Hurrying, I clattered up the ramp. The inside of the van was dark. Barrel Man tied the rope to a ring. For a moment, I was able to see the light-colored horse tied next to me. Her backbone stuck up, and her coat was dull, but when we touched noses, I knew it *was* Dappled Filly.

The ramp shut with a clang, and we were in darkness. We whiffled excitedly, but then the motor roared, the van lurched, and I spread my legs to keep from falling. We rumbled down roads for what seemed forever. Finally the van squealed to a stop.

I smelled horses. Were we back at Santa Anita? Would Lanny, Wolf, and Marie be there?

The ramp lowered, and light poured into the van. Barrel Man led me down the ramp. I blinked as I looked around, immediately realizing this was not Santa Anita. Turning, I looked for Dappled Filly. A groom was tugging her down the ramp. She walked carefully, as if her feet hurt. Raising her head, she whinnied at me, but her eyes were as dull as her coat.

"This steel-gray colt looks good," Barrel Man said, pointing at me. "Maybe he'll win a few. This light-gray filly, though . . ." He frowned. "Sweet Dreams. I'll bet she's done for."

Sweet Dreams. I like that name. I whinnied back at her, trying to tell her that it was okay, but the groom took her away.

Barrel Man led me into a stall. It was bedded with straw and the hay smelled fresh, but there was no Barn Cat, no Lanny, and no Stakes Horse. All down the shed row were claim horses, and it didn't take me long to realize that I was a claim horse, too, and that my life would change forever.

* * *

At Tanforan, I won my first race on a Wednesday and my second race on a Saturday. Strutting into the winner's circle, I was greeted with cameras popping. Not as many as before, but still, it felt good to be galloping and winning again. The only thing missing was a hug from Marie. But after my third race, when I walked from the winner's circle, a strange man took off my bridle and put a different halter on me.

"Risky Chance, you jest won me a hun'erd dollars," the man said as he spit something on the ground. "Tomorrow you'll win me a hun'erd more."

He led me to a different barn. A groom bathed me and walked me until I was almost cool, then tossed me in a stall. It didn't have straw bedding and the hay smelled musty, but I was hungry. When I poked my head over the stall guard, the horses on either side of me pinned their ears. Both had tired, hungry eyes.

I searched for Dappled Filly and neighed for Lanny. Nobody answered.

The next morning, a groom brought me a bran mash. My insides rumbled, and I ate every bite, licking the pan. At Santa Anita, mashes meant race day. Only I had just raced yesterday. Perhaps New Owner was nice after all and gave his horses mashes every day.

After I ate, a groom came in and brushed me until I shone. He combed my mane and buffed my hooves. *Not so bad*, I thought. Maybe I had lucked out with New Owner.

But that afternoon, the groom led me to the saddling paddock, and I realized this *was* race day. At Santa Anita, Lanny gave me lots of days to rest between each race. Obviously, New Owner didn't agree. In the saddling paddock, I saw the horse stabled on my right. When he walked, there was a slight hitch in his gait as if he hurt.

New Owner was there, talking to a jockey. "This horse won his last race," he was saying. "Push him to win. I've got big money riding on him." He handed the jockey a whip and boosted him into my saddle.

I eyed that whip. I felt the iron grip on the reins. I switched my tail to show my anger, but the jockey tapped me with the whip as if to show me who was boss.

The bugle sounded, we headed for the post parade, and I forgot about everything but *winning*.

Done For

Rain misted on us as we paraded past the grandstand. The track was soggy, but I didn't care. The field of horses would be easy to beat. Too many acted sore or worn-out. Then I spotted Dappled Filly. She trotted past me with high, frantic steps. Her eyes were white-rimmed.

As she went by, I nickered to her, but she seemed not to hear—or to care.

"Chance!" Someone called my name. I halted, sliding in the mud. A boy hung over the inside railing. He wore a cap and overalls. A short man stood beside him. His face was pale, and he leaned on sticks. Who were these humans? I lifted my head to catch their scent.

Whap! The whip struck me hard. "Git up!" the jockey growled, and I bounded forward.

I broke clean from the starting gate, but still the jockey whipped me. My ears pinned tight in anger, and I ran that race with only half my heart. Partly because I hated that whip, but also because of the heat that began in my leg. When I crossed the finish line in third place, I looked for Dappled Filly. She straggled in last. Foam dotted her mouth, and her head hung. What had happened to the high-spirited horse who used to race me neck and neck?

"Filly's done for," her jockey said as he dismounted.

I neighed, calling out to her, but she disappeared in the milling horses and riders.

New Owner's face was red when he hurried

up. "This horse should've won!" he exclaimed. "What in thunder happened?"

The jockey snorted. "He only came in third because the rest of the field was half-dead. I had to whip him four times. Something's off. You need to check his right front leg."

"Horse is as sound as my grandmother."

"Then your grandmother must use a cane," the jockey said as he dismounted and took off his saddle.

"Well, it doesn't matter if he is lame," New Owner said. "Horse won me some money, and he's been claimed. He's someone else's problem now."

And so, tired and sore, I was led to another barn.

I was hungry and sweaty after the race. But

a skinny groom about the size of a broom handle barely walked me, and the spray from the hose was cold. When he led me into a stall, I found old hay and no warm mash.

That night, another owner came in. Smoke swirled around his head. Bending, he felt my legs. "Horse is lame," he said gruffly. "I should have known not to claim a horse from that crook Bugsy. Ice him. Rub him with liniment. Wrap him. Hand-walk him tomorrow. And put some of this in his feed." He handed the groom a packet. "I want him racing sound in three days."

The skinny groom tried. But he was as hungry and tired as I was. He put the white powder in my grain but forgot to ice my legs. He slathered on liniment, and then wrapped the bandages so tight that my leg swelled.

The next day, Gruff Owner's shouting could be heard up and down the shed row. He cuffed the groom and told him to get packing. Then he wrapped the leg himself. "You're costing me money, horse," he muttered as he worked. Standing, he put more powder in my grain. It tasted bitter, but I was so hungry I ate it anyway.

On race day there was no mash.

For what seemed forever, I stayed in Gruff Owner's barn. On race days my legs were wrapped. I ate white powder in a handful of grain. Rarely did I get out of the stall for a gallop. Never was there sweet hay or kind words. My muscles grew stiff, my ribs thin, and I could barely stand on my right leg. I hadn't won a race in ages.

"You'll need to use this." Gruff Owner handed the jockey a whip for my next race.

"Horse is slow. He's got no fire. Only thing he'll understand is the sting of a whip."

"I'll make him run," the jockey said.

The jockey whipped me from the starting gate to the final pole. I crossed the finish line last. By the time the jockey dismounted, welts had puffed up on my flank and rump.

My head hung as low as Dappled Filly's the day she'd lost her race. Not because I was ashamed that I was last. Not because clods of dirt from the other horses had pelted me in the face. Not because my neck and chest were sweat-crusted.

I hung my head because of the emptiness of my heart. I no longer cared about winning.

"Thank the stars some sap finally claimed him," Gruff Owner said when the race was over.

"Lucky for *you*," the jockey told Gruff Owner

as he took off the saddle. "Not so lucky for the sucker who claimed him. This horse is done for."

Done for. That's what the jockey had said about Dappled Filly.

Gruff Owner pulled off the bridle and put on the halter. He led me toward two people coming onto the track. I recognized them. It was the short man who walked with sticks under his arms and the boy wearing overalls.

I turned my head away. By now I knew what would happen. I was a claim horse. That meant no special person owned me. Even worse, the man and the boy would soon discover I was done for.

What would happen then? What happened to horses who could no longer run and win?

I thought of Dappled Filly and shuddered.

"Chance!" The boy suddenly rushed toward

me. The cap fell off his head, and curls tumbled to his shoulders.

It wasn't a boy; it was Marie! She threw herself against me, her arms circling my neck.

"What in thunder are you doing to my horse, boy?" Gruff Owner snapped.

"I'm not a boy," Marie declared. "And this isn't your horse. It's ours. So please, sir, will you take off your halter so I can put on mine?"

By now the man with the sticks had hobbled toward us. He moved as slow and stiff as I did. When he drew beside me, I realized it was Wolf.

I greeted him with snorts of delight.

Marie hugged me again. "You're mine now, Chance. Father and I claimed you." Tears dotted her eyes as she ran her fingers gently over my welts. "No one will ever whip you again."

I heard her words, but only when she took off Gruff Owner's leather halter and slipped a rope one over my nose did I realize what they meant.

I was going home with Marie.

A New Owner

"Horse is all yours," Gruff Owner said to Wolf. "Too bad he's washed up."

Wolf's eyes didn't glow like Marie's, and there was worry in his voice when he said, "Believe me, sir, I know he's dead lame. But my daughter is convinced he'll be the next winner of the Santa Anita Handicap."

"Ha-ha!" Gruff Owner laughed so hard that smoke blew from his nose. Taking his halter, he hurried away. I was glad to see the last of him.

"Chance is *not* washed up," Marie said as she led me from the track. "You wait and see, Father."

Wolf shook his head. He walked slowly beside us, swinging those sticks. "I hope you're right, sweetheart, since it took the last of our savings to claim him."

Stopping, I nudged Wolf with my nose. I wanted to tell him how happy I was to see him and Marie. The nudge knocked one of the sticks, and he lost his balance and toppled to the ground.

"Father!" Marie kneeled to help him up, but he swatted her away.

"I'm fine. Take the horse to our gear. We need to wrap those legs before the walk home."

Marie was quiet as we made our way to the backside. I flicked my ears, wondering which barn I would go to this time. Would I be back with Tall Man's stakes horses? Would my new stall have deep straw and sweet hay?

Marie steered me behind the last shed row. There she pulled a sack from behind a scraggly bush.

Taking a rag from the sack, she wiped my sweaty saddle mark. Then she rubbed me all over, and my muscles felt less tight and achy. Once I butted her to say thank you, and she stroked my neck. But there was no noisy chatter like the old Marie.

She had changed. It was more than the boy's

cap and overalls. She was serious and silent compared to the magpie she'd once been.

Marie was almost finished wrapping my legs when Wolf finally hobbled around the corner of the barn. His face was pale, and he was breathing as hard as if he'd run a race.

"You need to rest, Father," Marie scolded. "We have a long walk home."

He sank against the back wall of the barn. "I'll be all right. Bill Steers offered to drive me."

Marie humphed. "You mean Bill, who, like all your jockey friends, never bothered to visit you in the hospital. *That* Bill?"

"Don't blame the other jockeys. They didn't want to see me busted up. They didn't want to be reminded that they could be lying in that bed, their careers done for."

I lifted my head. There was that term again.

"I'll only go with Bill if you'll be all right on your own," Wolf added.

Marie patted me, and I laid my muzzle against her shoulder. Her wraps and bandages were not too loose, not too tight. I put more weight on my right leg, testing it. It still felt sore, but so much better that I breathed a sigh.

"I'll be fine. I'll be with Chance," Marie told him.

Wolf swung his gaze to me. "I hope you're right."

"Mother and I were on our own almost a year while you mended," she said, sounding like a grown-up. "And I was fine when we had to sell everything to pay the hospital bills. Walking home is easy."

Wolf shook his head. "I don't mean about that. I mean I hope you're right about Chance. He looks almost as broken as me."

"You're not broken." Marie's eyes snapped. "And Chance is only broken because all his owners cared about was money. They never cared about him. Have you forgotten what you said when you two were winning every race? You said, 'That horse has more heart than any I've ever ridden.' We just need to help him find that heart again."

"I'm glad you're sure, Marie." Wolf smiled faintly. "I'll watch for you when I get home. Don't forget to bring the rucksack." Leaning again on his sticks, he headed off.

Bending, Marie loaded the sack and swung it over her shoulder. We headed down the dirt lane that wound past the barns. The sun was setting, casting a red glow on the backside. We passed horses being bathed and hot-walked and grooms cleaning saddles and bridles.

I was used to these sights. But when Marie led me to a gate that opened onto a wide road, I planted my hooves, not budging. Outside the gate, there were no green fields, no barns, no dirt tracks, no grooms, and *no* horses.

Trucks roared past, barely missing us. It was as noisy as if a race were being run, but I didn't hear music or "They're off!"

"It's a big world outside the track, Chance," Marie said. "You'll have plenty of time to get used to it. Right now we need to get home before dark." I felt a shiver run through her.

"People are so poor and desperate these days that it's not safe to be out alone."

Lifting one foot, I set it on the black road. My iron shoe clanked on the hard surface. Slowly, we made our way along the roadside. Trucks and cars rumbled past. A horn honked, and I jumped nervously. Finally we turned onto a quieter dirt road. We passed a field, but I couldn't see any grass, fences, or horses. Instead it was crowded with people.

"That's a Hooverville," Marie said. "Families live there in shacks, tents, or under the stars because they have no jobs and no money."

As we walked past, a herd of raggedy children ran up to me. They pulled at my tail and darted in to pat my side. "Can I ride? Can I ride?" some shouted. Others begged, "Can you spare a penny, miss? Please, a penny?"

Nervous, I scooted closer to Marie, who shooed them away with her hand. When we made it past the Hooverville, she said, "Times are tough for everyone, Chance. At least my family still has a home." She tipped her chin up to look at me. "Just don't expect a stall like the one you had at Santa Anita."

Dusk had fallen by the time Marie steered me down a grassy lane. It wound between olive trees, ending at a tiny house. I was so tired, my head was dragging.

Wolf met us, and without a word, the three of us walked around the house to the back. There was no fancy barn, no white board fences, no fields, no grooms, and no mares or foals grazing on a hill.

Marie led me into a tiny paddock under towering trees. In one corner were fresh hay and a bucket of cool water. Another corner was bedded with soft straw.

"I know it's not much. When we get the money, we're going to build a shed," Marie said as she unclipped the rope. I ambled to the hay and ate a few bites. Then I drank deeply. Weary, I folded my legs and plopped in the straw. Marie lay next to me and leaned against my side.

Fresh air ruffled her hair and my mane. Stars twinkled overhead through the leaves. Silently, Wolf watched us from where he leaned on the top fence board.

I heaved an exhausted but grateful sigh.

I was home.

April 1939

The dry hillside rose in front of me. Snapping my legs, I trotted to the top, where it flattened. There were few trees, and no holes and rocks.

Hunching low on my neck, Marie gave me my head. "Show me what you've got, Chance," she whispered.

I stretched into a gallop. *Faster. Faster.* The air beat against my face. Rocks shot from under my hooves. Balanced on my back, Marie was as light as a fallen leaf. *Run. Run.* This was the first time I'd galloped since my last race. Happiness filled me. I could have run forever.

Too soon Marie eased me to a trot. I heard her whoop like a child. "We won, Chance!"

Later we walked down the hill, cooling off. For three months, Marie had been riding me in the hills behind our home. We started off walking, then trotting. When my bow was fully healed, she'd started cantering me. Today, galloping in the warm spring weather, I'd barely broken a sweat.

"You're almost ready, Chance. I can feel it. It's like there's a motor roaring inside you. Like Father's car—the one we had to sell to claim you,"

Marie said, once again chattering like a magpie.

The wind swirled in the treetops, and I pranced sideways. I was ready to take off up another hill.

"You'll be ready in several weeks," Marie went on. Her hands were light on the reins when she steered me back to the path. Unlike a lot of other riders, she never kicked or tugged or whipped.

"I'd love to be your jockey, but I'm a girl." She blew out a breath. "Oh, I can work after school with Mother sewing doll clothes. And I can wrap your legs and clean your stall and exercise you. But *girls* aren't allowed to ride on the track.

"That means we need to find someone who will help you win your first race." Marie patted my neck. "Not the hundred-grander at Santa Anita. Father says the entry fee is too rich. But we'll find the perfect race and the perfect jockey."

We reached the dirt lane that led home. Behind me, a horn blasted. I leaped to the road-side. A line of trucks drove past. They rattled and spewed dust in the air. The truck beds were heaped as high as a mountain. Chair legs stuck

in the air. A woman with a baby was perched atop a mattress. Children were wedged between tables and quilts. No one waved as the trucks passed, as if all were too tired.

"Okies," Marie said. "Come from Oklahoma to California to find work. Most travel from farm to farm. They have no home."

I spotted our house through the trees. Lifting my head, I whinnied. Nanny Goat bleated back. She shared the small paddock. I was glad that I had a home, but sometimes I was lonely for another horse like Dappled Filly to talk to.

Wolf waved from where he stood by the gate. He still limped, but he no longer had to use the sticks. "How'd he do?"

"Six furlongs in one minute and twelve and a half seconds."

For a second, Wolf stared at his daughter as if not believing how fast I had gone.

"I'm teasing, Father," she said as she dismounted. Bending, she felt my right leg. "Cool and tight. He'll be ready to race in several weeks."

Wolf's face grew stiff. "I've entered him in a race for this Saturday, Marie."

"That's too soon!" She straightened so fast, she startled me.

"It's a four-thousand-dollar purse. That's more than I make at the factory in a year."

Marie propped her fists on her hips. "Chance isn't ready."

"I have no choice." Wolf blew out a breath. "Feeding him has been expensive. He needs to earn his keep. You said his leg is cool and tight, right?"

Marie continued to glare at her father.

"I'm sorry, Marie. The truth is we're broke. I spent our last money on the entry fee. We need this win or we lose everything. Tomorrow I'll go to Tanforan and check out the bug boys. We'll find a good jockey."

Frowning, Marie let her arms drop. "We'll *all* go to the track. You, me, and Chance. If he's gotta race this soon, he needs to help us pick his jockey."

"I know it would be better to wait." Wolf put his hand on Marie's shoulder. "But times are tough. With the purse money we can pay bills and maybe start building our barn."

"And we can claim another cheap horse," Marie suggested. "It'll be the start of our own stable. When Chance wins, people will see that you're more than a jockey whose career ended in an accident. You're a great trainer, too."

Wolf smiled. "You're the trainer, Marie. You took Chance from broken down to tip-top. Let's hope he wins Saturday. It's our only chance to keep going."

"Oh, he'll win," Marie said confidently. Turning, she ran her hand lightly down my neck. *"He will."*

The next day, Marie rode me to the racetrack. Wolf met us there.

We huddled on the outside railing, watching the morning workouts. My ears flipped as I took it all in. It had been ages since I'd galloped on the track, and my heart longed to be out there with the other horses.

"What do you think of the boy exercising the bay?" Wolf asked Marie. "He's a strong rider."

She quickly shook her head. "Too strong for Chance. See how the horse resists him?"

"How about the one on the gray filly?" He pointed to a horse galloping past.

I lifted my head to look, too. Instantly, I recognized Dappled Filly. She was more alert than the last time I'd seen her, but I saw sadness in her eyes.

"The horse looks like she's been pushed too hard," Wolf went on. "But the boy seems to be getting a decent ride out of her."

"You're right," Marie agreed. "I like the way he's talking to her. Chance?" She gazed up at me. "What do you think? Should we meet him?"

Just then, I heard humming behind me. I turned so quickly I tore the reins from Marie's grasp.

Lanny! Blowing excitedly, I pushed him with my nose. He laughed and ruffled my fore-lock. "I believe the horse hasn't forgotten me."

Marie gave Lanny a hug, and Wolf shook his hand. All three were grinning. "None of us could forget you," Marie said.

"What are you doing at Tanforan?" Wolf asked him.

Lanny tipped his head. His hair was as gray as mine. "When Chance left, something in me left, too," he said. "I couldn't bear to work with another great horse just to see him claimed or sold 'cause the owner was greedy. So I quit."

"You're too talented a trainer to quit," Marie

said. "But I understand. The only good thing about Davidson getting rid of Chance was that we claimed him."

Lanny grinned. "I heard. Any chance you'll be running him again? I've got money saved up for a bet." He rubbed under my mane

just like he used to, and I wiggled my top lip.

"He's entered in the fifth race on Saturday," Wolf said.

"We're picking out a jockey now," Marie said. "Do you know anything about that exercise boy?" She pointed to Dappled Filly's rider.

"That's Blink. The boy's so skinny, if you blink you might miss him. He's an Okie. Started riding in the bush leagues. Has a gift with horses, just like you, Wolf. He's a bug boy for Winston, who hasn't noticed yet how good he is. You might be able to get him to ride one race for you."

"Let's go talk to him," Wolf said.

We hurried to the backside. I tugged on the reins, eager to see Dappled Filly.

Blink had dismounted and was taking off the saddle when we came up. I greeted Dappled Filly with excited whinnies. "Why, these two horses must know each other," Blink said. He patted me, and I liked that he didn't jerk Dappled Filly away.

She was glad to see me, I knew, because she greeted me with whiffles of delight. "Dreams was foaled at Davidson's farm," Lanny explained. "Same as Chance. They used to race up and down the fence."

"Were you and Sweet Dreams friends, Chance?" Marie asked. "She sure is beautiful. At least she *was*. Based on the knots and splints in her legs, I'd say she's been run to death." Holding the cheek pieces of the bridle, she stared into Dappled Filly's eyes. "I'm sorry no one has loved you, Dreams."

Marie went back to talking with the others, and I laid my head over Dappled Filly's withers. She rotated one ear as if wanting to say hi, but then seemed to sag with exhaustion.

"What do we have here?" a voice boomed. A huge man, his buttons popping on his vest, strode toward us. Eyes squinted, he walked around me. Marie hurried over and placed a hand on my neck.

"I'd bet a day's wages this is Risky Chance," Huge Man declared. "Winner of eight straight stakes races at Santa Anita. I thought he'd been shipped to the packing plant."

Marie's face turned bright red. "He was not! He's fit and ready to win again Saturday."

"Marie, meet Mr. Winston, Blink's boss," Wolf said. "He's owner of the best stable of horses at Tanforan."

Huge Man didn't even glance at Marie, Lanny, or Blink. "And I aim to keep it that way. What race is Chance entered in?" he asked Wolf.

"The fifth."

"I got a colt entered in that race. Kingsman."

He stepped close to Wolf. Raising one hand, he poked Wolf so hard in the chest that he staggered backward. Lanny caught Wolf to keep him from falling. I laid my ears back, not liking the way Huge Man treated Wolf.

"There's no way a has-been like Chance will beat Kingsman. *No way*," Huge Man said, his eyes mean. "I'll make sure of it. Now leave my stables," he added before striding off.

"I believe that was a threat," Lanny said. "You best keep your eyes on Chance night and day."

Wolf nodded. His face was pasty white. "Well, Blink," he said, "I gather that means you won't be able to ride for us."

Blink threw an ugly look at Huge Man's departing back. "I'd be proud to ride Chance," he said. "Winston don't have a contract on me."

Wolf placed a hand on his shoulder. "Are you sure? Could mean trouble."

Blink snorted. "I'm an Okie. My family lost everything in the dust bowl. This here ain't trouble."

Marie gave me a smile and a pat. "Well, Chance, looks like we've got you a jockey." I bobbed my head, glad to see Huge Man gone and Marie smiling again.

"And a heap of a lot of misery, too," Wolf said. He rubbed his leg as if it pained him. "I'm afraid Mr. Winston will be gunning for Blink and Chance in the race."

"Let him." Marie tipped up her chin. "Chance will win, no matter the odds."

April 1939,
Race Day

Marie buzzed around me like a bee. Washing my tail, brushing my coat, braiding my mane. One of Wolf's friends had lent us a stall at Tanforan for the big day.

I hung my head over the door, goggling at

the swarm of grooms, riders, and horses. The noise and confusion excited me, and every time I heard "They're off!" blasting from the grandstand, I wanted to run, too.

Lanny came up, wearing a big grin. "You polish that colt any more, Miss Marie, he'll be bald."

"Chance might not have the fanciest tack," she told him as she trimmed a stray hair on my muzzle. "Nor the finest blanket. And he won't come from Winston's *best* stable." She spat the word. "But he'll be the handsomest. And the fastest. And when he wins, everyone at Tanforan will know that my father is the best trainer in California."

"That's a lot to place on the back of one horse," Lanny said as he scratched my withers. "What if he comes in second? Or last?"

Marie shot him a dark look. "He won't."

For a moment, Lanny was silent. Then he said, "You don't have to act so brave, Miss Marie. I know what's at stake."

Ignoring him, Marie bridled me.

"Your father told me you could lose your house."

She gave me one last swipe with a rag. Stepping back, she studied me. I arched my neck. "He'll win," she declared. "Mother and I saved every nickel we made from sewing those doll clothes. We bet it all, Lanny." Tears glimmered in her eyes before she brushed them away.

I felt her sadness. She reminded me of Dappled Filly, and I laid my head on her shoulder.

Crossing his arms, Lanny studied me, too. "Chance was the best colt I'd ever trained," he said quietly. "Before people ruined him. You've done wonders with him, Miss Marie. I do believe he could beat the moon today."

"He just needs to beat nine other horses."

Lanny nodded. "I'll meet you in the saddling paddock. It would be my honor to help send him off to the track."

"Thanks, Lanny." When he left, Marie stooped and ran her hand down my right leg. Was she worried about my bow?

Rising up, she laid her cheek against my neck. It felt hot and wet. Then, pulling a cap from her back pocket, she put it on and tucked in her curls. "It's time, Chance," she said, and, straightening her shoulders, she led me from the stall.

The saddling paddock was crowded with fine and fresh-looking horses. Tails switched.

A horse reared. Others kicked out, narrowly missing me.

Marie's mother waved a handkerchief at us from the crowd. Roses bobbled from the brim of her hat, reminding me of that long-ago day when I'd first met Marie. She blew us a good-luck kiss. Lanny put on the saddle pad and saddle and tightened my girth.

I spotted Huge Man. He stood by a tall, big-boned bay. He was talking to the bay's jockey. Instantly, I recognized Stubby. My nostrils flared, and I flattened my ears angrily. As the bay pranced and hopped, Huge Man glared at me and stabbed one finger in my direction.

Raising my head, I stood quietly. I didn't need to prance for the crowd. I wasn't frightened of Huge Man or Stubby, either. I'd been claimed by grumpy and gruff owners. I'd been ridden and whipped by too many jockeys like Stubby. I'd been treated like I was nothing and told I was done for.

Life had changed me as it had Marie, Blink,

Lanny, and Wolf. I knew what I had to do. First out of the gate. First against the railing. *Run. Run. Faster. Faster.* And never look back.

"Chance knows how to win this race," Wolf told Blink, who suddenly looked like a child. "All you need to do is listen to him. That's how we won eight races together."

"And no whip," Lanny and Marie chorused.

"Yes, sir, and uh, ma'am." Blink touched his hand to his cap. Lanny boosted him into the saddle. For a moment, Marie wouldn't let go of the reins. She stared up at me, and I could see worry in her eyes. Was she wishing that she was the one riding me today? Or was she worried I couldn't win?

"It's up to you, Chance," she said, and, letting go, she stepped back.

Blink steered me around the paddock, and then we followed the other horses onto the track. The bay was two ahead of me. Stubby turned in the saddle. Raising his whip, he smacked it sideways in the air as if hitting another horse's head. His eyes were on me. Then he grinned nastily, shifted his gaze to Blink, and slashed again with the whip.

I waited for Blink to tremble at the sight. But he only chuckled. "Stubby thinks he's scaring us," he said. "Only 'scared' is when the sheriff threw my family out of our home. 'Scared' is seeing my mom and baby sisters cry 'cause we had no place to live. A whip cracked across my face? That's nothin'." He whistled under his breath. "Kingsman, though. That's one ace of a horse. He'll be tough to beat, Chance."

Breaking into a jog, I caught up with Stubby and the bay. A mounted attendant held Kingsman's head, keeping him under control. His knees lifted smartly as he trotted past the grandstand. His tail fanned in the air, and he tossed his head, showing off as the crowd roared his name. Stubby waved, enjoying the attention, too.

"Odds are twenty-five to one on you, Chance," Blink said as we passed the totalizator board. "Kingsman's odds are three to one. Seems the crowd doesn't believe you'll win. I guess we'll have to show 'em what a long shot can do."

Nine other horses and jockeys gathered behind the starting gate. The assistant starters loaded us one by one. Horses were lined up on my right and my left. The last horse to load reared and crashed through the gate. I heard the bay snort. The horse next to me pawed nervously.

Finally the last horse loaded. Eyes wide, I watched the flagman. He raised his arm. Blink sat forward, his fingers clutching my mane. He was as chilly as I was.

The flag went down; the bell rang. Reaching out, I clawed the track with my two front hooves. I pushed off with my hind legs, powerful from trotting up and down the hills with Marie. I bounded from the starting gate before the others. In two long strides, I was against the rail. In four strides, I was ahead of the other horses. Blink rode like Marie: as light as a fallen leaf. I knew he was there by the slight pressure on the reins and the whisper of my name.

I hurtled around the turn to the backstretch,

nine horses close behind me. Nine horses that were waiting for me, the front-runner, to tire and fall back.

But the will to win raged inside me. It pushed me faster and faster down the back-stretch. Along the inside railing was a blur of faces and waving arms. Shouts rang in my ear, and I heard my name and then the name Kingsman chanted over and over.

As I neared the final turn, I cocked my ear, listening. *Huff, huff* came from close behind. The bay wasn't giving up. It was time to let him know who was the best.

I lengthened my stride and surged forward. All of a sudden, pain hit my right leg. Even with all Marie's patient care, my injured tendon wasn't holding up. I faltered. Blink must have felt my misstep, because he tightened the reins as if to ease me back.

Huff, huff. Suddenly, the bay was pulling beside me. I rolled my eye to the right. I saw Stubby's nasty grin. I saw him switch his whip to his left hand. I heard Blink's sharp intake of breath as the whip snaked out. Stubby was keeping it low so the stewards on their platform wouldn't see.

Stubby had steered the bay so close I was trapped between him and the inside railing. I couldn't swerve right or left. The only way I could avoid the whip was to outrun him.

I leaned into the final turn to the homestretch, trying to keep my weight off my right leg. *Crack!* The whip cut my ear. If I could just hold on, we'd soon be heading down the final stretch. Stubby would have to stop whipping because of the stewards' sharp eyes.

Run. Run. Faster. Faster.

Blood coursed through my muscles, spurring me on. I shut my mind to the pain spreading up my leg. The homestretch loomed ahead. Kingsman and I were neck and neck. As we thundered down the homestretch, the grandstand erupted. Were those Marie's and her mother's cheers I heard? Were those Lanny's and Wolf's shouts of encouragement?

I could never have heard them over the crowd, so I must have heard them in my heart.

Blink crouched lower. His hands rested high on my neck. I felt his courage and energy flow into me. As if we were one, we sailed toward the finish line. Kingsman still hugged my side, but he wasn't going to beat me. I would win for Marie, Wolf, and Lanny. I would win because *I would never race again.*

Calling on my last surge of power, I leaped forward. We passed beneath the finish line a nose ahead of the bay.

Instantly, Blink leaned back on the reins. When I slowed, he kicked his feet from the stirrups and jumped off. "Whoa. Whoa." He stumbled but didn't let go. Pulling hard, he got me to turn. My right leg seemed to buckle beneath me, and I almost fell to my knees. But Blink was there, pressing his weight against my right side, holding me up.

Then Marie and Lanny were there, too. Marie's face was smudged with tears. I searched for her smile. I had won, hadn't I?

She wrapped her arms around me. "Thank you, Chance," she said. "You made our dreams come true." Then as suddenly as she had arrived, she disappeared.

Quickly Lanny took off my saddle, handed

my reins to a strange groom, and hurried off. Confused, I searched for him. Blink and Marie's mother were helping Wolf make his way to the winner's circle. Marie and Lanny were nowhere in sight.

Turning away, I hobbled beside the groom, my head bobbing with each painful step.

Now I understood why Marie was crying. I had been claimed by a new owner. Not that I blamed her. I was truly done for. Even Marie couldn't keep a Thoroughbred that would never race again. I wouldn't be able to pay for my keep. I was no use to her and her family.

My heart was heavy as I limped off the track, but I never looked back.

It was later when the vet came into my stall.

I wasn't the only horse who'd broken down that day, so he'd been busy. Fortunately, the groom had taken care to untack me and cool and rub me down. He'd rubbed liniment on my leg and fed me a bran mash. But even the bran mash couldn't lift my spirits. Marie and Lanny were gone. I was once again a claim horse. And when the vet opened the door, I stood in the corner, my head hanging.

Bending, the vet inspected my leg and said to the groom, "I'm tired of patching up these horses so some money-hungry owner can race them one more time."

"Horse does act beat down," the groom said. "As if he lost the race instead of won."

"Yeah, well, that's 'cause his next stop will

be the packing plant," the vet said after he ran his fingers down my leg. "I don't know if I should waste bandages on him."

"You better," someone declared. Rolling one eye back, I saw Marie burst into the stall. "My horse just won us a pot of gold."

Lifting up my head, I took a sideways step toward the door. Why was she here? "A pot of gold, huh?" The vet instantly brightened. "That means I'll get paid for once."

Marie gave me a fierce hug. Then she held my head as the vet put a poultice on my leg. Still, I kept rolling my eyes at her, not sure what was going on.

"I'm sorry if you thought we'd abandoned you, Chance," she said. "Wolf and Blink had to talk to the stewards. Mr. Winston accused Blink of fouling Stubby." She made a disgusted noise. "We know *that* isn't true. Fortunately, the stewards knew Stubby was lying, too. And after your race, well, Lanny and I had something special to do."

When the vet rose to get wraps, Marie led me forward a few steps so I could see out the open stall door. "I had a plan, Chance." Her voice rose excitedly. "I knew what I wanted to do with Mother's and my winnings. Father doesn't even know."

Craning her neck, she looked up and down the aisle. I peered out the doorway, wondering why she was so excited. Then I heard humming and the sound of a horse's hooves thudding on the packed dirt. Lanny turned the corner, leading a skinny light-gray horse.

Sweet Dreams! Lanny grinned. "Glad to see

your old friend, I bet," he said when she and I touched noses.

Marie wrapped her arms around Dreams's neck. "I claimed her, Chance! Lanny helped me. She was in a race after yours. We had to make our claim in a hurry. But she's mine now. Mine!"

Dreams blinked as if confused. I was confused, too. Was I going home with Marie? Was Sweet Dreams coming with us? Why would Marie want us? As she had said earlier, Dreams was raced to death. And me, I would never race again.

"Oh, I have such big plans. Especially for you, Chance," Marie said. "When your leg heals and school's out, you and I are going to become mounted attendants on the track." She plunked her cap on her head so she looked like a boy.

"There's good money for a rider with his own horse," she went on. "And with my pay, and Mother's doll clothes, we're going to build a barn, because when Sweet Dreams gets her spark back, she's going to give us the first of many fine foals."

While Marie talked, Lanny listened and nodded. A grin stretched his cheeks. "I'm putting my winnings in with Miss Marie's," he said. "Soon our stable will be bursting with speedy two-year-olds. And with Wolf's and my training, Marie's riding, and Blink's expert jockeying, we'll be the top barn in California in no time."

Just then, I heard Wolf's voice. "The stewards fined Stubby," he called as he came up the barn, arm in arm with Marie's mother. Blink was

right behind them. He looked completely tuck-
ered out, yet his grin was as big as Lanny's.

Marie and Lanny went over to congratulate
them. The vet had finished and was packing
his bag.

That gave me a chance to talk to Dreams.

Once my friend had had a gleam in her eye
and a shiny coat and had been as fast as I was.
Now her eyes were hollow, her coat was ashy,
and she had no fire left. I knew that would
change. Dreams wore an old rope halter. And
when Marie took off the leather halter I wore
and put on my old rope one, I knew what that
meant, too.

I blew in Dreams's nostrils. I told her that we
were going home with people who would treat

us with kindness, who would love us even though we were done for as racehorses.

We were two of the lucky ones. We were no longer claim horses who belonged to no one.

We belonged to Marie.

APPENDIX

MORE ABOUT THE THOROUGHBRED

Thoroughbreds in History

About three hundred years ago, three Arabian stallions were brought to England from the Middle East. Their names were Darley Arabian, Byerly Turk, and Godolphin Barb. They were bred to the larger, heavier English mares. The new foals had strength and speed. They were called English running horses. Later, they became the first of a new breed called the Thoroughbred.

In 1764, Eclipse, a great Thoroughbred, was born. He was named for the eclipse of the sun that happened that year. He won eighteen races. About 95 percent of Thoroughbreds can trace their roots back to Eclipse.

Bulle Rock was the first Thoroughbred brought to the United States, in 1730. Kentucky, with its rich bluegrass and mild climate, became a center for Thoroughbred breeding and racing. Racing continued in Kentucky even during the Civil War.

Thoroughbreds Today

Thoroughbreds in the United States and Canada are registered with the Jockey Club, which was formed in 1894. Each horse receives a unique name, such as Valentine Lassie, Zee Bird, or The Mad Artist. Today there are about 445,000

names in use. Every Thoroughbred racehorse's upper lip is tattooed with a unique number. But all Thoroughbreds have the same "birthday," January 1, no matter when they are born.

Most Thoroughbreds are bred for racing. They have large nostrils and lungs for deep, strong breathing. They have long legs for fast running. The famous racehorse Man o' War had a stride of twenty-eight feet! Thoroughbreds are noted for their speed, reaching up to forty miles an hour.

The Thoroughbred ranges in height from 15 to 17 hands. (A hand measures four inches.) A grown horse weighs between 900 and 1,200 pounds. Thoroughbreds' colors are brown, bay, chestnut, black, and gray, with some roans.

Not all Thoroughbreds are racehorses. Some

are bred and trained for jumping and dressage. Others compete in steeplechase and polo. Temperament often decides what a horse is best suited for. Thoroughbreds can be flighty but often possess great heart.

More About Life During the 1930s

Risky Chance is set during the Great Depression. This period began in 1929 and didn't end until America went to war in the 1940s. Banks crashed. Businesses went bust. Fathers lost their jobs. Families lost their homes.

Children like Marie had to go to work to help their families. They strung safety pins on cords, sewed buttons onto cards, or put bobby pins in packages. They could earn about two dollars and

fifty cents a week. A family was considered rich if they earned six thousand dollars a year. Most families, however, earned about four hundred and fifty dollars a year. During the Depression, many could no longer pay the one-dollar electric bill. "For a whole week, we didn't eat anything but potatoes," one child said about his life during the Depression.

More About Racing in the 1930s

Horse racing became a popular sport during the Great Depression. By 1935, two-thirds of homes owned a radio. (There was no television.) Families loved sitting around listening to a dramatic horse race or baseball game. In 1934, Santa Anita Racetrack opened in California. It offered a hundred-thousand-dollar purse for the winner of the Santa Anita Handicap race. Today that would equal seven *million* dollars!

During the Depression, Seabiscuit became a popular horse hero. Huge crowds swarmed the racetracks to watch the crooked-legged Thoroughbred run. He was featured on the covers of *Time*, *Life*, and *Newsweek* magazines. Just as in *Risky Chance*, Seabiscuit raced Rosemont in the 1937 "hundred-grander" and lost by a nose.

Horse racing has always had claiming races and stakes races. In a claiming race, all the horses in the race are for sale for the same price. Before the race, a buyer may claim (buy) the horse whether it wins or loses. A track official will tag the horse, which will then go to its new owner. In stakes races, the horse cannot be claimed.

Racing is exciting but also dangerous. In the 1930s, jockeys did not wear protective helmets or vests. The tracks did not have ambulances or safety rails. Nineteen jockeys were killed between 1935 and 1939. Like Marie's father, many more were injured. Racing is safer today, but it is still a dangerous sport. Between 1992 and 2006, twenty-six jockeys died, according to the National Institute for Occupational Safety and Health.

Racehorse Rescue

There are many risks for racehorses as well. Thoroughbreds often begin their racing careers as two-year-olds. They can break down in training or, like Risky Chance, be injured during races.

Greedy owners who are only interested in winning may race older horses with injuries such as sore ankles.

The American Society for the Prevention of Cruelty to Animals (ASPCA) was formed in 1866 in New York City with a full-time staff of three. Henry Bergh was the driving force behind the organization, which then focused on horses and livestock. In 1867, the society operated the first ambulance for horses and provided fresh water for the horses that pulled streetcars in Manhattan. Soon humane societies were formed in Buffalo, Boston, and San Francisco.

Today there are many wonderful organizations that specifically rescue racehorses. They can retrain the horses so they may go to pleasure riders, sport riders, and families. Some of these organizations are CANTER (canterusa.org) and Thoroughbred Adoption Network (thoroughbred adoption.com). You can find more about these groups on their websites.

⇜ COMING SOON! ⇝

Northern Nevada, 1951

Black Cloud is a black-and-white mustang colt. He loves roaming free with the rest of his herd, playing with the other foals, and learning the ways of wild horses. But when humans intrude on his wandering life, Black Cloud's world is changed forever. Here is Black Cloud's story . . . in his own words.

About the Author

Alison Hart has been horse-crazy ever since she can remember. A teacher and author, she has written more than twenty books for children, most of them about horses. She loves to write about the past, when horses like Bell's Star and Risky Chance were valuable in everyday life. Her novel *Shadow Horse* was nominated for an Edgar Award. Today Ms. Hart still rides, because—you guessed it—she's still horse-crazy!

About the Illustrator

Ruth Sanderson grew up with a love for horses. She drew them constantly, and her first oil painting, at age fourteen, was a horse portrait.

Ruth has illustrated and retold many fairy tales and likes to feature horses in them whenever possible. Her book about a magical horse, *The Golden Mare, the Firebird, and the Magic Ring,* won the Texas Bluebonnet Award in 2003. She illustrated the first Black Stallion paperback covers and a number of chapter books about horses, most recently *Summer Pony* and *Winter Pony* by Jean Slaughter Doty.

Ruth and her daughter have two horses, an

Appaloosa named Thor and a quarter horse named Gabriel. She lives with her family in Massachusetts.

To find out more about her adventures with horses and the research she did to create the illustrations in this book, visit her website, ruthsanderson.com.

Collect all the books in the Horse Diaries series!

Elska

CATHERINE HAPKA
Illustrated by RUTH SANDERSON

Bell's Star

ALISON HART
Illustrated by RUTH SANDERSON

Koda

PATRICIA HERMES
Illustrated by RUTH SANDERSON

Maestoso Petra

JANE KENDALL
Illustrated by RUTH SANDERSON

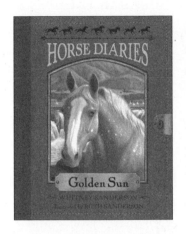

HORSE DIARIES

Golden Sun

WHITNEY SANDERSON

illustrated by RUTH SANDERSON

HORSE DIARIES

Yatimah

CATHERINE HAPKA

illustrated by RUTH SANDERSON

⇒ **And coming soon!** ⇐

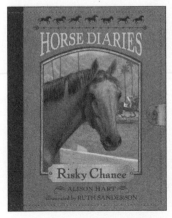

HORSE DIARIES

Risky Chance

ALISON HART

illustrated by RUTH SANDERSON

HORSE DIARIES

Black Cloud

PATRICIA HERMES